The Bla‹

What readers say:

'I couldn't put it down!'
Alice Lindsay, 9 years old

'This is an amazing novel.'
Betsy Davidson, 10 years old

'This was the best book I've read this year.'
Eva Valentine Niespolo, 9 years old

'... It's alright.'
Kev Thorne, age unknown

Dedicated to the children of Strand On The
Green Junior School

Contents

Chapter 1

Rotten Luck

'It's not fair.' words that are spoken daily, but how much truth is there to this statement? It's certainly difficult not to sometimes feel cheated when everyone around you seems to have everything, and you're left with very little. At least that's how ten-year-old Arthur Morgan felt, cheated, resentful and often left out.

'James, please stop, just go to sleep,' said Arthur.

'I'm sorry; I'm just so excited! It's sports day tomorrow!' replied James. It's times like these when Arthur wished he had his own room. Arthur lived with his mum, dad and younger brother James in London.

They lived in a tiny flat so small that he shared his bedroom with his brother. Sharing a room with his five-year-old brother definitely wasn't Arthur's idea of fun. He couldn't complain too much, the flat was so small, Arthur's mum and dad had to sleep in the living room.

The flat was right next to The River Thames, with amazing views to wake up to every day. Every morning he could peer out the window and see rowing boats and the local sailing club. 'I can't sleep with all this noise downstairs, this is ridiculous' moaned Arthur. Unfortunately, it was also above a popular restaurant, which meant a good night sleep was never easy.

Arthur's mum called from the living room,

'Don't worry boys I'll sort it out, just do your best to get some sleep.'

Arthur thought his mum was some kind of superhero; she fixed everything and did things so fast without complaining once. She was a court stenographer, the person who types everything everyone is saying in a courtroom. Arthur thought this is how his mum got things done so fast. Within minutes the whole flat felt silent again. Arthur's dad was still working. He worked strange hours and Arthur never quite knew exactly what his dad did, only that when there was noise from the restaurant downstairs, his mum would be the one to make it stop.

Arthur didn't have a terrible life; he had a roof over his head, clean clothes and a loving family. But then so did all of his other friends, only thing was, they all had a lot more. They all had the latest video games, Arthur didn't, they all had the latest mobile phones, and Arthur had nothing. Whenever there was a school trip, Arthur had to pretend to be sick so his friends didn't know the truth that his parents just couldn't afford it.

Arthur always tried to be positive about things, focus on what he did have instead of what he didn't, although some days it could be difficult. Mondays were usually frustrating. His friends would come back from the weekend having a great laugh about something they were all talking about in their group chat. When Christmas was approaching, that was awkward. Everyone guessing what they would be getting for gifts and Arthur knowing it would just be essentials for him, mainly socks and a second-hand toy that would have been the best Christmas gift five years ago. Arthur Morgan definitely said the phrase 'it's not fair,' on several occasions but today everything was about to change.

Chapter 2

Walk To School

'Arthur!' his mother yelled, 'get out of bed right now and don't make me come in here again!'

'Can I just go to school on my own and leave in half an hour?' mumbled Arthur.

'You know the rules, now get up.'

'This is so unfair.'

Arthur could have stayed in bed a little longer, but his mum and dad had to leave for work, and he was too young to be home alone. Luckily they let him walk home on his own after school, as they were always back by then. This meant he didn't have to walk with his brother which was a relief. Slowly rising out of bed, Arthur got dressed for school; curtains still shut, lights off, so his eyes didn't have to deal with the blinding sunlight just yet. James was already up and couldn't wait for school to start; Arthur was definitely feeling the complete opposite.

Stepping out of his room, Arthur felt his stomach drop, the thought of going to school terrified him some days,

'I don't feel well,' murmured Arthur.

'Nonsense, you'll be fine once you've had breakfast, come and sit down.' Mum said brushing off his failed attempt of escaping school. Arthur sat down, folded his arms and rested his chin on his arms, looking as miserable as ever. Luckily, Dad had just finished work and burst through the door.

'Dad!' yelled James running to give his dad the warmest of welcomes. Arthur didn't move an inch, still feeling the same knot in his stomach. Arthur's dad laid a gentle hand on Arthur's shoulder, and asked with his heavy Irish accent, 'Hello cheerful, what's up with you?' Arthur hesitated for a moment, he was about to try the same sob story on dad but thought it would be a waste of time.

'Nothing, just tired that's all' said Arthur.

'Ay I tell you what,' dad began nudging Arthur in the shoulder until he made eye contact with him,

'If you come home tonight, with no detentions and a smile on your face, then we'll go straight to the park and play football. What do you say?' Arthur couldn't hold back the smile from his face. He loved going to the park to play football.

'OK, I'll do my best, but my stomach really does hurt, and you know I have history today.'

'You'll be fine once you start eating, now hurry up or we'll be late.' said mum.

Arthur's mum and dad didn't even entertain the comment about his history lessons; they were frightened of his teacher Miss Madison as well.

'Can we go now?' asked James.

'Hang on, let me finish my cereal,' said Arthur, he resumed his rapid eating and was almost done.

Upon leaving the house, Arthur had another panic, 'Wait! My homework, one second,' cried Arthur, he would have hated to turn up to Miss Madison's lesson without his homework.

'We are definitely going to be late' said James.

Off they went, out the door, James running ahead, Arthur dragging his heels with their mum caught in the middle, shouting for one to slow down and the other to speed up. As they walked, all at different speeds, Arthur thought back to the times he enjoyed school. It wasn't that long ago, only this year did he really start to despise the idea of being in the classroom. The constant humiliation and torture his history teacher put him through.

'What do you mean you don't know? Wake up!' was Miss Madison's favourite line. There were plenty more. 'Are you listening, or should I shout louder.' One time she caught Billy with his head on the desk. Instead of tapping him on the shoulder or shouting, she smacked a ruler on the table, missing his head by just a few inches. After Billy jumped up from his chair, Miss Madison leaned in as if to whisper but instead screamed, 'Oh I'm sorry, did I wake you!'

Arthur hated History for this reason. He loved everything else, Science, Maths you name it. Arthur's passion was anything to do with global warming. He'd spend hours reading and watching clips online about amazing new technology that could save the world from the mess it was in.

'Hurry up, Arthur, you're going to be late.' Mum called, snapping him out of his reverie. Past the train station they went, James was still skipping ahead but being told to slow down every ten seconds. Arthur hated living in such a small flat but loved where he lived. Right next to the River Thames but most importantly, just two minutes away from the railway tracks. Arthur loved trains and was fascinated by how fast they could go.

'Mum, did you know the bullet train in China travels over 200 miles an hour!' said Arthur finally starting to pick up the pace, so he could tell mum more.

Just passing the local train station, the boys spotted the same person who always greeted them, a small man hunched over sitting on nothing but cardboard outside the station.

'Any spare change Miss,' said the man directing his attention to Arthur's mum.

'I'm afraid not today, sorry.' replied Arthur's mum keeping her head down, like so many adults who strolled past the man.

'No problem, have a good day Miss, and you boys.'

Arthur felt frightened; he didn't say a word back, but just cowered behind his mum. The man posed no threat, but strangely, Arthur couldn't help but fear the unknown. Why was this man on the street?

'Do you think I'll win my race Arthur?' asked James, changing the subject. Arthur remembered how excited he used to get over sports day. 'Of course,' Arthur said proudly, 'and even if you don't just make sure you beat Suzie Brunel, can't stand her brother, David.' James couldn't help but laugh, 'OK, I'll do my best!'

Arthur hated David, he didn't always hate him, and in fact, in infant school, they were quite close, not anymore, not since David started playing more football and less time doing anything else. David became obsessed, if you were no good at football, David had no time to talk to you. A part from when he needed your help with work. This made Arthur despise David even more. He would bully Arthur until he gave him all the answers. Then David would make sure Arthur was never a part of the football games at lunchtime. Thinking about it, Arthur wasn't sure whom he hated more, David, or the dreadful Miss Madison.

Chapter 3

Miss Madison's Morning

Rising out of bed sharply, no alarm clock needed, Miss Madison emerged from her cold, hard bed, ready for the day ahead. She stared into the mirror, straightening her hair with a faint smile on her face. It was unclear at that moment, with the sinister look of seriousness on her face, whether Miss Madison was preparing to go to work, and teach history to a group of ten-year-old children, or preparing to fight on the battlefield with the world at war.

Miss Madison lived all alone and liked it that way; other people were a distraction to her and her work. Her work was the only thing she cared about. While getting changed, Miss Madison realised a small mark on her white collared shirt. 'Not good enough,' she said to herself, putting it to one side, and found an identical one. Of all the different words Miss Madison's students would use to describe her, she knew the best one. Perfectionist. 'If you can't do it right, don't do it at all' or another she often told the children, 'Good enough isn't good enough, if it can be better.' Miss Madison demanded the very best of herself every day and insisted that her children did precisely the same.

All changed and hair neatly put in a bun, Miss Madison was all set to leave the house. But something was different, once she stepped outside; the scene was entirely different from Arthur's. There was a lot more hustle and bustle around the streets of London. Miss Madison also lived by the River Thames, in fact just down the road from where Arthurs address would be.

The only difference was, Miss Madison was living in the 1800s! No cars on the road or planes in the air, just horses and stagecoaches.

Walking through Victorian London was also soothing for Miss Madison. Despite being overcrowded with beggars, pickpockets and the police doing their best to keep the peace, she always managed to find some kind of calm amongst the chaos. A combination of the fact she had grown up on these mean streets and was immune to the despair all around her and that fact she knew she wouldn't be around these parts for very long.

Within no time at all, she arrived at the school gates, two hours early as usual. She waved hello to the caretaker of the school grounds on the way in, oblivious to that fact this was her first interaction with a human all morning. Interestingly, the caretaker was the only man to know why Miss Madison came to the school so early. She was not there to teach the children at this nasty ragged school, but just to use one piece of equipment. She continued down the dark, dusty hallway. No artwork hung up or children's achievements on the walls, just the plain light blue painted wall with a noticeboard at the end of the hallway. Turning into the classroom, Miss Madison now took a deep breath to prepare for her trip she had made a thousand times before. Despite taking these trips countless times, she always felt the same knot in her stomach every time.

Picking up a piece of chalk, as elegantly as a painter picks up their brush before creating a work of art, Miss Madison wrote on the blackboard the date, not today's date but a date that will live long in her memory, almost a couple centuries into the future. Before leaving, she had one more job to do. 'Neil, my dear, could you do me the honours?' Miss Madison called down the hallway. Neil, the caretaker, came running down the hall, eager to assist Miss Madison in any way he could.

'Yes certainly madam, be safe over there.'

'I will don't you worry, just make sure you use the eraser here and don't get any of the chalk on your hands,' Miss Madison handed him the felt eraser for rubbing out the date once she had left, to avoid anyone from her time following her. Miss Madison didn't trust many people, but she always trusted Neil.

Within seconds of touching the white chalk on the blackboard, the chalk did not wipe, away but began to illuminate, and in a flash, Miss Madison vanished from Neil's sight. 'Still spooks me no matter how many times I see it,' Neil said, talking to himself. He did exactly as he was instructed to do; he rubbed the date out and left the room at once. Moving on down the hall with his mop and bucket, Neil still wondered how it all worked, was it the blackboard or the chalk that was so unique? Still muttering to himself, he decided one day he'd have the guts to ask Miss Madison.

Chapter 4

Last Minute Homework

Getting to the school gates just in time for the bell to ring out, Arthur said goodbye to his mum with just a smile and a quick nod, trying to stay cool in front of his friends. He ran a few yards ahead to chat to one of his classmates, Tom. 'I can't stand Mondays, an hour of history!' said Arthur.

'I know, did you finish the homework?' said Tom.

'Yeah, wasn't too bad, still won't be good enough for Miss Madison though. What about you?'

'No, I was too busy this weekend, so I didn't have time, not looking forward to seeing her face when I have to tell her.'

Arthur felt a sharp pain in the pit of his stomach once again; obviously, Tom didn't have time, he was probably on his phone chatting to his friends all weekend. Meanwhile, all Arthur was doing was some pointless history homework about the boring Victorians.

'My dad said he'll take me to the park later if I have a good day, you want to join in?' asked Arthur eagerly wanting Tom to accept.

'Sorry Arthur, doubt I'll be able to escape early enough from here, with no homework, Miss Madison's definitely going to give me a detention.'

'I'll come with you later Arthur,' Said a voice behind the two boys, it was Lucia, one of the best footballers in the school.

'Oh, um, well, yeah OK thanks Lucia, I'll knock for you later,' said Arthur trying his best not to seem nervous, Lucia was always kind to Arthur, but he was still shy around her. 'Great, see you later,' said Lucia. She then ran ahead to speak to another one of her friends.

Arthur now couldn't wait for the school day to end, where he'd finally be free. All he had to do is keep quiet and not get in any trouble, a task that was really easy for most but no one was safe if they had Miss Madison that day. Lucia would be safe; she had Mrs Granger all day, one of the happiest, helpful teachers in the school, 'So unfair,' Arthur whispered to himself.

Trudging up the stairs as slow as they possibly could, so Arthur and Tom could avoid every second of being in that classroom. Suddenly, the boys were surrounded by a colossal shadow following behind them. It was David Brunel, the mean, horrible boy who had been tormenting Arthur since the school year began; the boy was huge in height and width, with dark brown hair slicked back. He put on a lot of weight recently, but not fat, even though he was just ten, David looked like a fifteen-year-old who had been going to the gym after school every day. David's physical appearance made everyone around him feel weaker and less important as him. The worst part of all was that he knew it and in fact, he loved it. 'Hey Archie,' David said knowing this always infuriated Arthur, 'I need that homework again. I was at the park all weekend playing football. Well played by the way Tom,' Arthur turned to Tom with a guilty expression on his face. 'Thanks for the invite' Arthur groaned.

Tom tried to defend himself, 'It wasn't planned, someone put it in the group chat and it just kind of happened.'

'Listen we're wasting a lot of time, Miss Madison will be here any minute, either give it to me or I'll just have to take it,' said David with his hand out, but the rest of his body, stood like a boxer, legs stretched shoulders apart, ready to pounce on Arthur any moment.

Arthur stood still for a moment not sure whether to give David all his hard-earned work, or take the risk, that David was just pretending and would never actually lay a hand on a boy he used to call his friend. Arthur had no choice in the matter; David grabbed his bag right off Arthur's shoulders, unzipped the bag with a flick of the wrist and yanked the homework out from his school bag within seconds. Once the homework was safely in David's hands, he pushed Arthur to the floor to avoid any chance of Arthur snatching it back. Tom stood still as a statue the entire time not sure whether to run or help Arthur, instead, his body chose for him, he didn't move a muscle and David didn't lay a finger on him. Arthur got to his feet, defeated and once again whispered the same thing he always did in these situations, 'This is so unfair.'

Chapter 5

In Trouble Already

Stepping into Miss Madison's classroom was like stepping outside on a freezing cold winters day. There was very little colour on the walls and only the basic notice boards around the room, Maths, English and Science. No artwork or children's achievements were anywhere to be found, just like it was in Miss Madison's classroom back where she came from. The room lacked personality and smelt of bleach. One thing was sure; it was the tidiest classroom in the school. No scuff marks on the tables, not a single pencil misplaced and just an old blackboard in the corner of the room that Miss Madison used a lot more than the smart board that was placed in the centre of the room. Arthur thought the blackboard was probably twenty years old, but it was spotless, no faint chalk marks from previous lessons. In fact, if a stranger walked in, they would think it was brand new.

A voice echoed around the room,
'Right, water bottles on the side, come and sit down at once, ready for registration,' There she was, standing there with the best posture anyone had ever seen, with her long black ankle-length skirt followed by a tailcoat jacket with that white collared shirt she had to replace. Arthur always thought she looked like an evil version of Mary Poppins. Someone who spent most of their life treating children like unwanted flies that just can't escape the room. 'I hope you all had a productive weekend and didn't just spend it all playing silly games,' shouted Miss Madison with a disdain for anything involving fun. No one spoke, they all sat silently waiting for the next instruction, worried they would do something wrong if they moved an inch.

'What are you waiting for?' said Miss Madison, 'don't just sit there, write the date and title!' just a few seconds in and she was already angry with the entire class. It didn't matter what subject Arthur was doing with Miss Madison, all he could think about was History after lunch. If Arthur didn't get his homework back, then he would be in detention and lose the chance to play football with his family and Lucia. Countless scenarios played out in his head, could he sneak into David's bag if he asked to go to the toilet? Pointless, Miss Madison never let anyone leave the room in the middle of a lesson, during lunch? No way. Miss Madison would be patrolling the hallways at that time. 'Arthur, what do you think?' said Miss Madison. Arthur was panicking; he was so busy daydreaming of ways to retrieve his homework, he had completely zoned out. 'Well, Mr. Morgan... it's not a rhetorical question, I demand an answer!' yelled Miss Madison. 'I...um...I... I don't know.' Arthur said feeling his face turn bright red from embarrassment. He looked around the room to see if anyone could help, all he could see was Tom looking just as puzzled and David smiling, trying his best not to burst out laughing but still making himself known to Arthur that he loved every second of this. 'Well then, this is your final warning, if you slip up one more time, then you will find yourself in detention.' She said this with an almost hopeful look on her face.

Arthur thought she loved punishing kids more than she enjoyed teaching them. At that moment, Arthur hated David more than ever before; he wouldn't be daydreaming of getting his homework back if it weren't for David taking it in the first place. After lunch, David would have single-handedly landed Arthur in detention. Arthur felt hopeless but did his best to try and ignore the eventual doom that was awaiting him after lunch and focus on not getting another answer wrong.

Once the morning was over, Arthur had managed to keep himself away from trouble, but there was no escaping it, Arthur went off to lunch and felt sorry for himself all break time. Tom tried to cheer him up by inviting him to play football, but Arthur politely declined. Nothing could cheer Arthur up at this point. He sat on the steps, just thinking of what to do. 'You OK Arthur?' a voice came from behind him, it was Lucia again, with her friend Sarah. 'Not really, looks like I'm not going to be able to go to the park later.'

'Why not?' asked Sarah, hoping she could join them?

'Miss Madison is going to give me a detention for the homework that's due.' Said Arthur still looking down at the playground surface.

'Oh no, you didn't do your homework?' asked Lucia.

'I did but… it's a long story,' Arthur was about to tell the whole story but could feel a tear coming from his eye. He chose to avoid answering so the girls wouldn't have to witness Arthur crying his eyes out. The bell rang abruptly around the school, and it was finally time for Arthur to face the music, or in his case, the wrath that was Miss Madison! 'Sorry again, Lucia, hopefully, another time?' asked Arthur.

'Of course, just let me know when,' said Lucia with an innocent smile on her face, trying to hide her disappointment.

The journey from the playground to the classroom felt longer than ever, and yet Arthur didn't want it to end, mostly because he knew what was awaiting him. The humiliation of being singled out in front of the whole classr was just seconds away, and Arthur had run out of ideas.

'Right then, before we start our next subject on Victorian society, let's have everyone's homework in about the industrial revolution.' Arthur's face changed colour again, turning red hot and felt his vision go blurry. Before he knew it, tears were starting to fall from his eyes. He buried his head in his hands and rested his head on the table. Arthur Morgan looked pitiful, but Miss Madison took no notice at all. 'Where is your homework, young man?' asked Miss Madison. Arthur raised his head in fear but realised she was speaking to Tom. 'I didn't do it, I'm really sorry Miss' said Tom.

'Right, well then, I'll see you in detention after school today, and I expect it in tomorrow, or I'll keep you after school every day this week until it's handed in!' Miss Madison was now in front of Arthur's table,

'Here you go miss,' said David, handing Arthur's homework in with an arrogant look on his face. You could still see the faint markings of where David had rubbed out Arthur's name and replaced it with his.

'Thank you David, and yours Arthur? Where is it?' Arthur thought about telling the truth that David stole his homework, but he knew that wouldn't benefit him at all. Miss Madison wouldn't believe him, and David would get his payback at some point, and that frightened Arthur more than anything. It was safer to just take the detention and live to fight another day.

'I didn't manage to finish it in time,' said Arthur in a quiet mutter.

'Detention for you too then! If there's one lesson you lazy kids all need to know it is this, the harder you work, the easier life is.' Arthur couldn't help but feel angry; he wanted to stand up on his chair and scream. What a load of rubbish Arthur thought, I worked hard and did my very best, but David was being rewarded for it. Arthur had spent hours on that homework, and there it was in Miss Madison's hand, except David would be getting all the credit, yet there he sat awaiting his detention in two hours. All Arthur could think about was how unfair this all was, he wanted to run out the classroom, straight to the toilets where no one could see him, and cry till there were no more tears to be shed. But as usual, there was no escape, he had to sit and endure another lesson with Miss Madison, trying his best to listen to a subject he didn't care about.

Chapter 6

Detention

Arthur spent the rest of the school day thinking about the injustice of the situation and how wrong things had been. Even during his science lesson, which he loved, he struggled to focus without the thought of David stealing all his hard work; he couldn't stop thinking about what Miss Madison said about hard work. How long would this continue? Why should he work hard, while someone else could take the credit, what was the point? Maybe if Arthur had a phone, he would have been with David on the weekend, playing football, then he wouldn't be so cruel to him at school.

At that moment he felt anger towards his parents. Everyone else in the class has a phone, why couldn't he? It's not just unfair but it's embarrassing and pathetic. Arthur loved his family but he couldn't understand why he had to suffer through all this when both his parents get to have a phone. At one point he thought his little brother James would get a phone before he did!

3:20pm came, and it was time for Arthur to report to detention. One silver lining would be he wasn't alone, Tom was there, and in fact, so were five other children. It seemed Miss Madison really loved to punish these children. Detention was a cruel waste of time. Arthur would sit there for an hour with nothing but non-fiction books to read. Miss Madison said novels were for children who could escape from their current location and imagine a beautiful world, a world of endless possibilities. That would not happen in detention. If you were in detention, you deserved to stay in there, no escape, only the thoughts and regrets of why you were there to keep you company. Therefore, Arthur chose one of the several books Miss Madison had on the Victorian era. As much as Arthur read about how awful the children of Victorian London were treated, he couldn't help but laugh at the fact none of them ever met the evil Miss Madison.

Time seemed to go agonisingly slow. Arthur was trying his best to keep his head down to avoid further punishment. He tried to read the book in front of him, but then he'd look around the classroom to see how others were spending there time. Most were reading or writing, 'What on earth do you think you are doing!' Miss Madison screamed at the top of her voice, replacing the wall of silence with an explosion of noise that echoed around the classroom. Arthur looked terrified, what had he done that was so shocking to Miss Madison? 'If I see you looking around the classroom for someone to mime things to again, you'll be here every night this week!' Arthur didn't say a word, he just returned to his book, cowardly looking down at the pages in front of him, frightened that even saying 'OK' or 'sorry' would be the final blow Miss Madison needed to put him in detention for life.

Arthur had practically finished the entire book before Miss Madison dismissed everyone. Finally, they were sent on their way. The day had felt like a full week to Arthur, but now, he was free to go home. Still worried about being told off, no one said a word until they were outside in the playground, on the way to the school gates. 'Guess you're not going to the park now?' Asked Tom.

'Doubt it, I'll have to explain my detention to my parents tonight,' said Arthur looking pitiful. 'Are you going straight home?' Asked Tom.

'Yeah, have no choice, it's getting late,'

'I'll walk with you,' said Tom.

After an awkward silence between the two of them, Arthur had to address something that had been bothering him all day.

'You know you could have just knocked at my door if you were going to play football all day,'

'Arthur you live by the river, the park is half an hour away, I wasn't going to walk all that way just to see if you might want to come.' said Tom.

'Ok that's fair I guess,' said Arthur reluctantly shrugging his shoulders, but something was wrong. The weights of his shoulders were light, a lot lighter than before school, something was missing. Then he realised something terrible! He had left his bag behind in Miss Madison's classroom. 'I've got to go' said Arthur, he panicked and started to run back to school.

Chapter 7

Job Done

After a tough day of answering silly, unnecessary questions from children was exhausted. She never cared about giving children detention, if anything, they just kept her company while she spent the hour marking all the books she had the kids write in for the day. Miss Madison thought back to a simpler time, where children just wrote on slates, it was more environmentally friendly but importantly, a lot less marking. Finally, Miss Madison was ready to leave. Sadly, Neil, the caretaker, couldn't help her with erasing the date once she had disappeared. This was

Fern's job now. Fern knew the rules. Just wipe the blackboard clean every day after school with an eraser, never her hands. Fern once asked Miss Madison why the random dates but she was always shut down, 'please ask no questions, it's just my one wish that you do this, no fuss, can I trust you,' would always be Miss Madison's response. Clearly, Miss Madison just didn't trust Fern as much as she did Neil. This could be the fact that she's known Neil longer, or that Neil and Miss Madison come from the same time.

Once again, Miss Madison began to write, perfectly legible, 23rd May 1852. She looked up at the clock in the centre of the room impatiently, 'oh come on where is that woman, always late,' said Miss Madison under her breath. She always waited for Fern to be close by, to avoid anyone coming in before Fern managed to rub off the date. Ironically, Miss Madison had all the time in the world but had given up waiting. She knew that Fern would be coming passed shortly like she always did; Miss Madison would just have to trust her.

After one last look, Miss Madison had made up her mind; she was leaving now, no matter what. With slight apprehension, Miss Madison started to brush the date away with her fingers, but of course, the chalk did not disappear but began to light up once again, and a split second later, she was gone.

Chapter 8

Time To Panic

Sprinting as fast as his legs could carry him, Arthur ran past the busy streets of people just finishing work, dodging and zigzagging through everyone to get to school before it was all locked up. Some of Arthur's worst fears were popping into his head. He needed his bag otherwise all his notes on the homework would be left in school, and he'd have to pick it up tomorrow. If this were to happen, then there would be no way Arthur could do his homework tonight, which meant another detention tomorrow! Then thought he might get detention for life just for leaving his bag behind in the classroom, Miss Madison hated 'classroom clutter' she'd call it.

Trying his best to be as polite as possible when running past people, but inevitably bumping into them as they were all on their phones. Arthur eventually reached the school gates but sadly, it was too late, the caretaker was just locking up. 'Please Miss, I need to get in and grab my bag, please,' Arthur begged.

'How long will it take,' asked the Fern.

'No time at all I promise,'

After an uncomfortable silence, the caretaker gave into to Arthur's pitiful panicking state. 'Oh OK, but be quick!' said Fern tapping her watch.

'Thank you so much; I'll be a couple of minutes. Promise!'

Arthur raced up the stairs like his life depended on it. He burst through the door to find his bag waiting at the back of the classroom; Arthur drew a long sigh of relief, and it looked like Miss Madison never saw the bag sitting there under his desk. Arthur Morgan had done it. No detention for Arthur Morgan tomorrow he thought. With an infectious smile and a spring in his step, Arthur went to leave the classroom. But something felt strange, maybe it was because Arthur had never been in class alone, without a teacher in the room, it felt quite spooky.

Nevertheless, something was definitely different; upon leaving, he spotted something quite odd on the blackboard. It was blank like Miss Madison always left it except for one thing, the date, but not today's date. The blackboard read '23rd May 1852.' Arthur assumed this was a prank from someone in detention, some awful joke that being in this classroom reminded them of the vile Victorian era. One thing was clear; Miss Madison would not be amused coming in tomorrow and seeing this on her blackboard, and with the way Arthur's day went with Miss Madison, it would come to no surprise to him, if he was the first person on the suspect list.

Arthur had to do something to save himself from another detention. Searching for the eraser, Arthur began to worry; he only had a minute before the caretaker would get impatient. He decided to break another annoying rule of Miss Madison's, 'Never erase anything off the blackboard with your bare hands.' Arthur had no choice he needed to remove the random date and get out quickly. Arthur hopped on a chair and began rubbing out the date, but something strange started to happen. Instead of the date smudging and eventually fading away, it began to glow. Glow so bright that Arthur couldn't keep his eyes open. The blinding light was too much to bear. Arthur jumped down from the chair but the light grew brighter and brighter until Arthur could see nothing but pure white light, he was no longer in a classroom, but in a strange dimension that was pitch black, followed by a huge scream. Eyes closed, covering his ears with his hands and curling up into a ball, Arthur was in trouble. 'Stop, stop, make it stop!' screamed Arthur. Just when Arthur felt he couldn't take anymore, everything stopped. No light, no noise, nothing. Arthur slowly got to his feet and started to look around. Except Miss Madison's classroom looked very, very different.

Chapter 9

Lost

Arthur gazed around the classroom; there was no longer a smart board at the front, no tables grouped together, no books in the corner. Everything seemed to have changed apart from the blackboard still remaining spotless in the corner. There were tables, but they were in rows, similar to the style Arthur remembered taking his exams in. Just when he thought Miss Madison's classroom couldn't look more lifeless, it had become even worse. The entire room had an essence of complete misery, this was no place for a young child, Arthur couldn't imagine a single joyful memory that could take place in such a desolate, dark room. Arthur was perplexed, what should he do? He had no clue how to return to his horrible yet improved version of the classroom.

Arthur's heart was racing; he could hear footsteps echoing through the empty hallway. Someone was patrolling the school and was about to come across Arthur at any moment. Arthur stood frozen with fear of to whom the footsteps belonged to.

'What are you doing here?' said a strange man in a very old fashioned suit. He wore a top hat and had rather long sideburns. Waddling over to Arthur, cane in his hand, 'Well... answer me!' shouted the man impatiently.

'I just came back to get my school bag... but... now I'm not sure where I am,' said Arthur uncomfortably. The man took a deep breath and with a vicious smile said 'if you would like to play games, then let's play' throwing his cane to the floor, the man picked up Arthur from his armpits, roughly carrying him down the hall, while Arthur kicked and screamed, 'let me go, you can't do this, you crazy old man!' said Arthur close to tears now. At first, Arthur was anxious and afraid, but now he was full of anger and rage. Sadly, he was too small and weak to fight this giant beast of a man. The complete stranger kicked open the door to the main exit of the building, then, swayed Arthur back for a second, so he could be launched over the steps of the building. Arthur landed down as hard as he possibly could, straight into the puddle of muddy water on the street.

Arthur was in shock; no adult had ever handled him like that, with no care whatsoever for his well-being. Where was he? Why was the man so angry with him? What had he done to deserve this? Arthur got to his feet slowly, flicking the mud off his hands like a dog trying to get dry. When Arthur looked up to take in the scenery, he almost fainted.

What should have been a colourful modern London setting was something very different. The streets were packed with thousands of people, all wearing very old clothes. Horse and carriages, stagecoaches spread throughout the roads. Dark smoke covered the skies with a horrible substance of smog. The noise was deafening, with a tumultuous combination of beggars shouting for handouts, street merchants hawking their prices, and drunks starting fights outside what looked like old bars. But one sense stood out for Arthur more than anything, the smell. The stench was one of the worst experiences Arthur had ever had to endure. Countless horses meant unbelievable amounts of horse manure were left in the middle of the street. The smoke of burning tons of coal was seeping into Arthur's lungs, making him cough uncontrollably. Raw sewage seemed to flow through the gutters that would eventually reach the River Thames, the same river Arthur loved to wake up to every morning. What was usually the lifeblood of the city, now smelt like the river of death. The people on the streets gave off a hideous odour like they hadn't had a shower in months. Arthur was starting to feel very sick and was struggling to hide his revulsion any longer.

He ran down an alleyway for some privacy, and to gather his thoughts, but before he could do anything, he needed to be sick. Arthur gagged for several moments, but just when he was about to feel some relief, a horribly, dirty man covered in black rags, grabbed him by the shoulders and threw him to the ground. This time not landing in muddy water, but what had to be horse manure, making his school clothes unrecognisable.

'Argh! I'll kill you!' shouted Arthur, seeing red and trying to get to his feet but slipping. Arthur had finally lost his patience and wanted to get out of this horrifying place. The man began to laugh and said with a satisfied look on his face, 'don't you ever try to hurl down my parts ever again, go on! Get!'

Arthur got to his feet and decided this was a fight he was not going to win. Therefore, Arthur walked away but still confused as to where he was. Just when Arthur thought things couldn't get any worse, he sat down in the middle of the street and felt the first raindrop, the first of many. Within seconds it started to pour down. What should have disguised the smell, sadly, only made things worse. It was a disgusting, vile addition to the already overflowing gutters. Wet, cold, and miserable, Arthur was at a loss as to how to escape this terrible nightmare.

Chapter 10

Worst Night Ever

Arthur spent most of the evening thinking of ways to get back home. The only possible answer would be to get back to that classroom. There was no use trying to break in tonight, early morning would be Arthur's only option. This meant spending a night in this awful city. The local park offered little comfort in comparison to the streets. Everywhere Arthur looked he saw entire families sheltering under trees. The views he had seen of the backbreaking daylight were replaced with the misery of a dark night of despair. People looked down at him like a piece of gum stuck to their shoe. Arthur received nothing but dirty looks and mean faces as he walked through the park.

Arthur knew he'd be fighting for a sensible place to sleep, so rather than risk-taking someone else's home for the night, and causing a fight, he chose a small patch of grass in the open. His fear of causing any trouble outweighed his need to be kept warm by the shelter of a tree or park bench. Now that he had found a place, and no one had kicked him out of it, he finally felt his heart rate slow down. Although he felt more at ease, he was far from feeling safe and sound. Under the cover of darkness, Arthur finally thought he was able to cry, without fear of judgement from anyone else; this also gave time for Arthur to reflect on his situation. Arthur was all alone, in a place he had never been before, surrounded by horrible people, who treated an innocent, scared little boy like a dead rat found in their house. Wherever Arthur was, this was no place for a child.

As Arthur wept and shivered all night, all he could think about was how much he would love to be back home, in his tiny little flat in London, sharing his small bedroom with his little brother. But more than anything, he dreamt of having a shower. The thought of feeling that steaming hot water land on his head and fall down to his shoulders was the only thing keeping him from freezing to death. He had to keep moving while he laid down on the uneven surface of the grass. As the hours drew by, his desire turned to his bed, his beautiful warm single bed, waiting for him at home.

At that moment, he somehow resented the times he had struggled to sleep in it. If Arthur had those two pillows and a thick cover over him right now, he'd fall asleep in seconds.

Arthur wasn't used to living in this universe, he could peer around the park and see children the same age as him, truly living hand to mouth. Not knowing where there next source of food would come from, most had older people with them, probably their parents, but still Arthur felt like this was a world where everyone looked hungry, tired and miserable. The sun was beginning to appear behind the endless amounts of dark smoke that was ever-present in this place. Before trying to attempt a break-in at the building that threw him out yesterday, he needed to get some food. Arthur looked at where he could get food from, as he walked the streets of the over-populated town. He could see some children running around begging strangers, some who looked like they didn't belong in the same street as these poor children. Some were wearing the most glamorous top hat and cloaks Arthur had ever seen. And yet they choose to walk the streets with the families begging on their hands and knees for just a few breadcrumbs. Arthur was hungry, but he hadn't reached this stage of desperation just yet.

'Oi give it back, thief! Thief!' Arthur heard an old man shouting from behind him. He whipped round in a panic just in time to dodge a girl a little shorter than himself sprint past him, but in doing so blocked the man chasing her.

'That little rat just stole half a loaf from me, why didn't you stop her!' Arthur was offended at this elderly man, expecting him to play policeman for him.

'I didn't do anything,' said Arthur.

'Exactly my point, I'm getting the police. Clearly you and that rat are working together, and you blocked my path completely.'

Arthur had to act fast; he chose to run, run away from yet another adult handling him like a stray cat. He ran as soon as he could, but with no food to use as energy, he felt faint, running away, but only a few streets down until he gave up and finally hid down an alleyway. Panting with his head in his hands, he couldn't believe how easy it was to find trouble here. 'Thanks for that,' came a voice in the dark crevice one of the buildings in the alleyway, Arthur wiped the sweat from his forehead and squinted his eyes to see who it was. It was the same girl who ran past him. Just as he was about to explode, and blame her for everything that had just happened, she broke off a generously sized piece of her loaf of bread she had stolen and offered it to Arthur. Without a seconds thought, Arthur had calmed down and taken the piece of bread and started to waffle it down. Just when he was almost finished he looked up and said 'Thank you,' but the little girl was nowhere to be seen. Arthur looked in all the directions she could have gone in, but there was no sign of her. Fortunately, Arthur didn't mind, he finished his bread, which was the most basic breakfast he had ever had and was ready to sneak back into the classroom and do whatever he could to return home.

Chapter 11

Discovery

Arthur needed to get back to that classroom and from there, decide how he would miraculously return home. He walked on with purpose, not wanting to stay in this place any longer. Arthur thought his appearance would be a problem, but it seemed there were plenty of other children who had just come from working in the fields with muddy knees and many others who were covered in soot in the early morning. Everyone but Arthur seemed to be oblivious to the wretched smell that was lingering on the way to the schoolyard. Wasting no time at all, Arthur stormed through the crowds of children gathering up waiting for the school day to start.

So far, so good, no one had seemed to give Arthur a second glance. He seemed to fit in just well, but not everything would come so easy. Just as he was approaching the main doors, that hideous man came out from the other side, the same man who had thrown Arthur out the building only a few hours ago. He came waddling out still with his cane, inspecting the children as they walked into the ragged school. For a moment, Arthur thought, why does he even need a cane? The monster threw him out without a single limp yesterday. Just when he thought he could sneak past, Arthur locked eyes with him. 'You again!' said the man furiously stamping his cane to the ground. 'Wait!' pleaded Arthur 'please, I just want to get home, I'm lost, please don't hurt me.' The man hesitated for a moment and then decided to take a gentler approach.

'Fine, but what do you want here?'

'This is the only building I recognise, I've been coming to this school for four years,'

'Young man, this school has only been open for two years.'

'Wait… sorry sir, what's… the…?'

'Stop mumbling boy and get off my property,'

'Wait… where am I?'

'London, England, you fool.' The man said sharply.

Arthur was stunned.

'Now, are you going to leave or do I need to hire some of Queen Victoria's guards to stand here all day from here on out?'

'Queen Victoria? Oh no! No, it can't be,' Arthur was starting to piece things together, and just when he thought he'd figured out what had happened, there was a short and sharp sound that snapped him out of his daydreaming. It was the school doors being shut in his face.

Arthur was walking slowly, but his mind was travelling at a thousand miles an hour. How could this be? What happened? Time travelling wasn't really possible. Was it? Arthur was beside himself with utter sadness. He didn't cry, tears were replaced by an aching feeling in his stomach; Arthur wanted to cry but couldn't. Maybe if he cried, this horrible pain would go away. Everything was starting to make sense, Arthur had learnt a lot about the Victorians having Miss Madison teaching him. The thousands of people crammed into a small area, sleeping in streets and the park, urbanisation Miss Madison called it. Thousands of people moving from the countryside to the city for better work opportunities. Arthur couldn't pinpoint the exact date, but then he remembered, the answer popped into his head, like when you figure out the answer just after the teacher tells the class, the feeling of knowing but not being able to do anything a bit. 1852. The date that he touched on the blackboard. After learning this, Arthur felt far more alone than he ever did, being as far away from his family as humanly possible. This was a cruel trick to play on him, he thought. The one subject he hated, he was now living in it, every second, with no end in sight.

Chapter 12

Settling In

Arthur went to sit in the park to ponder his options; should he attempt another way into the school? Was there any point? Even if he managed to get back to the classroom, there was no instruction manual on how to get back home. The more he thought about it, he imagined the old man again, the thought of him catching Arthur a third time on that property terrified him. Now that he knew where he was, he knew the man wouldn't hesitate to harm Arthur again. Right now, none of that mattered. The main worry was how Arthur was going to find his next meal, and he hadn't eaten a proper meal for a while now. There were only two options that he witnessed looking around the streets earlier this morning, beg or steal. Arthur was never going to steal so it would come down to swallowing his pride and having to beg strangers for anything they were willing to give him.

So there he was, a boy who was used to showering every day, having three meals a day and a home to return to... now, looking strangers in the eye and pleading with them to give him just a penny or a piece of fruit. Arthur had always thought he came from a working-class family, but this was entirely different. This was now living hand to mouth, and doing whatever it took to survive.

After three hours of constant begging, Arthur had raised four pence, not much but enough for some bread. There were plenty of street vendors flogging their fees all around London, but Arthur just had to avoid one. Although this was the same location where Arthur walked the streets every day, he still felt lost.

One thing that was the same was the River Thames. Although the smell and appearance of the water was completely different, he would use the weaving river to guide him to where he needed to go. As long as he was near the river, he had a rough idea of the landscape. All Arthur wanted to do was sulk and scream 'this isn't fair!' but he knew this would get him nowhere; he needed to be proactive. He found an old lady selling bread just by the train station, Arthur always loved trains, but this was very different. He sat down and ate his food as slowly as he could to make it last as long as possible. Upon leaving, his curiosity got the better of him and had to ask,

'Excuse me, how old is this station?'

'Why it's brand new,' replied the old lady, 'Kew Bridge station is just about three years old now.'

Arthur sat there, still in disbelief; he had travelled in time, but not to the hopeful future. No, this was to the bleak past. He'd do anything to be walking along the River Thames right now, with his family, sun shining. Instead, he was sat on the cold hard floor, outside the station, where he walked past a man begging him for spare change, just twenty-four hours ago. This thought stung Arthur more than anything. He vowed that if he ever made it home, Arthur would give that man all of his pocket money he had been saving. No one deserved to live like this.

Arthur glanced around the streets to see if there were children doing things he could do. He had read in Miss Madison's books all the jobs boys used to have as a job in this period, chimneysweeper, factory worker or farm worker. Arthur had no experience with any of these jobs but would have to try, or he'd eventually end up in a place more depressing than this, the workhouses. No place for an innocent child, this is where the poor, or the orphaned children would go. They would do jobs to earn their keep and in return, be given food to survive. This was precisely what Arthur needed at this moment, but the only problem would be getting out. Once you were in, there was very little you could do to get out.

One man said he'd give Arthur two shillings a day, although this was ideal for Arthur, one chimney-sweeping boy took him aside and told him to run, the man was a liar, he promised the boys that, but only gave them one shilling a week! He wandered into a small factory where he saw boys a little older than him entering. Unfortunately, a man pulled him aside before he could even enter.

'You don't work here, do you, boy?' said the man, who already knew the answer to that question.

'No, but I'd like-'

'Get away! Don't need no waifs and strays round 'ere, go on! Away!'

Arthur ran without a further a seconds thought. No matter where he went, there was just no place for him. Arthur needed money for food, and he needed it now. Sadly, he landed in the worst place possible for work, thousands just like him were fighting for the same thing he needed most.

Chapter 13

Curious George

Meanwhile, George was finishing up the last bite of his lunch. Walking through the streets of London, he needed to get back to work. George was a navvy, short for the navigators who built the navigation canals at the very start of the industrial revolution. He was a short-haired, very tall, but baby faced man, whose heart was certainly bigger than his common sense at times. George had been working as a navvy since he travelled over from Ireland ten years ago before The Great Famine began. He loved being a navvy. Though dangerous, he enjoyed getting his hands dirty every day and playing such a vital part of building Britain.

George didn't want to be late, but he just loved the diversity of the big city. London had everything, the hustle and bustle of people running off to their jobs, the upper and middle class near those who had nothing. Everywhere you looked told a story, the fantastic display of gentlemen walking along, smoking their pipes. It really was a sight to see, one that George loved to visit whenever he could. Usually, George would be so amazed by all the commotion that he'd barely take a second look at the poverty that surrounded London. But today, something struck his eye or someone...

On his way back to the station, George couldn't help but feel pity for one boy, sitting alone, with the weight of the world on his shoulders. There were beggars on every street corner, but George thought something wasn't quite right with this boy. Beggars always had a sense of acceptance yet, resilience in their eyes, almost an 'I know I have nothing, but I'm going to do whatever I can to survive,' this boy looked dreadful, the absence of hope in his eyes physically hurt George. He couldn't just leave him there, something in George's heart told him; this boy didn't belong here.

'Everything OK son?' George asked in his usual strong Irish accent, not knowing if the boy would even look up.

Arthur's heart skipped a beat, just for a moment, he thought he had heard his dad's voice calling out to him. He looked up with such hope but was met with more heartache, eyeing up at a complete stranger.

'Not really,' said Arthur, while a single tear ran down his cheek.

'Hey, hey it's OK, how long you been out here, you look freezing cold. You got anyone? Friends? Family to help ya?'

'It doesn't matter. My whole family's gone, I'm all alone.'

George felt his whole body shiver when Arthur said these words. George had seen siblings, mother and son and many more suffer in the cold but never seen this, a boy, so young, so alone, with nothing but negative thoughts to keep him company. George's kind heart jumped in before his logical brain could stop him from speaking. 'Listen, if you really are all alone, then come with me, my boy's about the same age as yourself, could use a friend these days,'

Arthur had to think it over for a moment. Arthur knew never to trust strangers. But just as he was about to decline, George spoke once again. 'Listen, I don't have much to offer, but I get just under a kilogram of meat a day, it's not much but-

'OK,' snapped Arthur, he hadn't eaten properly for hours now, and the thought of meat in his stomach overruled the idea of anything that could be worse than this situation he was in.

As risky as it may seem, Arthur was no longer thinking the way of a boy raised in the twenty-first century, he was homeless, starving and hadn't spoken to a single friendly face for quite some time. Off they went,

Arthur finally having someone to talk to in what felt like weeks.

'Where are we going?' asked Arthur.

'Back to work for me, by the tracks, I'm a navvy so can't spend too long here. Got to get back to building Britain,' George said proudly while winking at Arthur.

'Navvies, are you the men who built all the railway lines?'

'Building still, yes it's been going on for years, but the business shows no sign of slowing down.'

Arthur was finally felt comfortable to squeeze out a smile from the side of his cheek.

'Wow, I can't wait to see you all at work, can I help?'

'Being a Navvy is a man's job, One day maybe, when you're a bit taller, I reckon you could be a great navvy.'

They spoke for a long time. Finally, for the first time, Arthur was starting to feel his heart slow down. George had managed to calm his nerves by just talking to him.

Chapter 14

First Warm Welcome

George and Arthur got to the railway line, and in no time at all, Arthur was introduced to George's son, John, a small boy not much taller than Arthur, but certainly a lot skinnier. Arthur couldn't help but stare at the hundreds of men working like clockwork, so the trains could run along these very hills for decades to come.

'Where are your parents then, Arthur?' asked John.

'They're out there somewhere, just don't know how to get to them' said Arthur, finally expressing some optimism.

'Ah well, nice to have some company while you figure things out' said John.

After some food, Arthur and John sat blissfully watching the hardworking men lift tons of muck while a handful of horses carried it away. The process was slow, but you could see the plan was coming together. Arthur had never seen the starting point before. The men would take a completely flat surface, and from there, they dug, and dug, until the flat field, was like a 'V' shaped hole, where the tracks would be right at the in the middle at the bottom.

'Where's your mum then?' said Arthur.

'She died just a few years back, just got sick, not sure what from, dad doesn't like to talk about it.'

Arthur felt a stabbing pain in his chest, he was overwhelmed with sorrow for John, and he couldn't imagine living his life without his mum by his side. Arthur felt hopeless just being away from his mum for almost two days now since she dropped him at the school gates. 'I'm sorry, I didn't mean to upset you, that's awful.' John was confused; he still had his father in his life. Arthur had no one. Why did he feel sorry him?

'Not that bad, you'd have to be one of the lucky ones to have both parents looking after you around here. Arthur had another reflecting moment; he'd been so fortunate to have two parents that love him, he wished he could show John how things have changed in his time.

There weren't many kids around the navvies, especially where they were working, in fact, it was mainly lonely men ensuring the railway lines were developed on time. Children and families were seen as a liability around this dangerous profession, and the other navvies weren't best pleased with George's decision to bring another child along the journey. 'You'd bring back half the London workhouse you would Georgie,' said Pat, one of the heaviest men working with the navvies. 'I couldn't leave him, Pat, you shoulda seen him, never seen such a poor face, so lost.'

'Well he's not having any of my servings, that's for sure.'

'Don't worry, the boy is my responsibility, just look at John, haven't seen him this happy since...' George thought back to when John's mother was still alive. This thought still hurt George more than anything. Even some of the happy memories still stung when he thought about them.

'You OK Arthur?' asked John.

'Yeah, just a bit cold still,'

'Don't worry, you'll get used to the great outdoors in no time.'

That didn't comfort Arthur all that much; he knew his history quite well. During this time, 250,000 navvies were employed to build the railways. This meant sleeping conditions were tight. They lived in shantytowns along the bridges and tunnels. They were just made of unused wood, which were moved down the road every mile when the workers moved on. Arthur took in the views of the hills, soon to be all dug up, this reminded him of the summer days his family spent in the countryside. Apart from the bone-chilling cold, he could close his eyes and imagine being back there.

Chapter 15

Life As A Navvy

Two days had gone by, Arthur was still settling into his new life as a Victorian boy. His stomach always craved more food than the usual bits of meat handed to him by George in the evenings. And he was barely able to sleep in the huts George made for him and John, He'd start to doze off when a cold wind would cut through the gaps in the wood, and Arthur would be wide awake again.

'Arthur!' a voice rang out in Arthur's head; he shot upright out of his sleep as his mother's voice echoed around the hut. Sadly, it was just a dream. Arthur was still far, far away from his family.

Just as George was about to get to work, John was pleading with him, 'please let me help today? You promised weeks ago you'd let me help, soon, you said,'
'You're still too young John, stay with Arthur, you can play on top of the hills where it's flat. Don't come down to the bottom.

John wanted nothing more than to be a navvy, to be just like his dad, but George knew how dangerous the job was and tried to keep John far, far away from the barrow runs and most of all, the building of the tunnels. This was the most dangerous place to be of all, digging and working underground, with nothing but candlelight's to help see what's in front of them. The only problem was keeping the naked flames away from the dynamite that was kept in the tunnels.

'Let's play over the hills John, I'll race you later!' said Arthur eagerly trying to keep John away from George's work. He knew the horrors that transpired down in those tunnels from reading Miss Madison's books. It was estimated that a man lost his life for every mile the navvies built.

After lunch, John and Arthur were exhausted from running around, climbing trees and seeing who could throw a stone the furthest. Arthur needed to sit down, but John still wanted to go one more place, down the tunnels. Arthur insisted it was a bad idea and would never go near the tunnels. 'Just come and see the entrance, they can go on forever but can just see a tiny light at the end.' said John.

'No way, never, I already told you, just come and lay down.' Arthur was halfheartedly pointing at the stump next to him as he laid his head back against the oak tree. 'This place is amazing, can you believe how quick these guys dig, with nothing more than a shovel and a pickaxe...' Arthur waited for a response, but there wasn't one. He lifted his head and looked all around him, John was nowhere in sight. 'John!' Arthur cried out, but there was no reply.

Arthur started running down the hill, searching for any sign of John, after five minutes, which felt like hours, Arthur had no choice but to go and look for John near the tunnel entrances. Running in a panic, Arthur ran into Pat, 'Oi, what you doing down here!' yelled Pat.

'It's John, I can't find him anywhere,'

'I don't care, if you two wanna play hide and seek, do it somewhere else!'

'He said he wanted to go to the tunnels, I told him no, but I can't find him anywhere! I think he's gone-'

'Out of the way,' Pat interrupted now sharing the same concern as Arthur. George was on the other side of the tunnel, so the men could meet somewhere in the middle.

Pat and Arthur ran like their lives depended on it. At that moment, they were shocked by a huge eruption! The sound echoes for miles and miles, every man around Arthur was covering their ears, a horrible whining came ringing out in Arthur's ears. Stunned and confused, Arthur dropped to his knees. The navvies went running towards all the commotion. They were met with the sight of men all throwing rocks out of their path furiously. The tunnel had collapsed in on itself. This was horrifying to see, George was in the tunnel at the time but so was John, along with fifteen other men. Arthur was screaming, 'John!' slowly, the men managed to pull out a few men who had survived the blast.

Limping forward, covered in earth and soil, barely recognisable John emerged. 'John!' Arthur repeated this time in a joyful way instead of a panic. John was alive, but all he cared about was getting some water and seeing if his dad was OK. 'I'm fine Arthur, honestly, close call but I'll be fine.' said John. Sadly, the same could not be said for five other navvies. 'You fool! I told you not to go near the tunnels!' shouted Arthur. But John wasn't listening; all he cared about was finding his dad.

Once Arthur had calmed down, he felt the same determination to see George. Just when they started to worry, George came stomping down the hill from the other side of the tunnel. 'What happened? I said no dynamite, we were practically metres away from you guys, you coulda killed us.' George's anger turned to complete despair when he looked down at John's muddy appearance. 'Oh, my word! What happened!' cried George.

'I'm fine, I was just near the entrance,' said John defending himself. George's anger returned like a man possessed. 'I told you never to come near the tunnels, get back up that hill at once!' John and Arthur ran up that hill, less out of George's request and more from fear he'd run after them and do something horrible.

Later that night, the boys sat under the fire with George giving them the bare minimal bits and pieces to eat. 'You boys scared the life out of me today, please just listen, when I say keep away from the tunnels, I mean.' George wasn't lecturing them, but rather kindly reminding them that what he does wasn't fun, or a game, but a serious life and death situation.

'We promise,' said Arthur nudging John on the arm who was staring at the ground.

'We promise,' John repeated.

'Good, especially tomorrow, the boss will no doubt be travelling down to inspect the mess we made today, terrible thing what happened to those lads.' There was a cold meaningful moment of silence the surrounded them. George broke the uncomfortable silence 'right, best get some sleep, big day tomorrow.'

Chapter 16

Isambard Kingdom Brunel

Dawn broke out, Arthur had the best sleep since arriving, and all the hours of worry had turned into acceptance. He hadn't given up on escaping this place, but he felt less alone having George and John with him. His only regret was not being able to earn his keep, although, he was far from offering any help, especially after what had just happened to John. The tunnel collapsing yesterday was a close call, but now the navvies had to explain what had happened to the engineer. Arthur and John were told to stay away from the situation, and that's precisely what they did, both climbed as high as they could up the oak tree, where they could see the engineer and a few others with him arrive at the tunnel. The man wore a big trench coat, an unusually oversized top hat, with muttonchops running down below his ears, which seemed to be the fashionable facial hairstyle of this century. He stepped out of his stagecoach, smoking a cigar, hands on his hips. The man presented himself with absolute importance.

'How could something like this happen?' exclaimed the engineer. Directing his anger towards George. George welcomed the man with open arms, happy to be in such presence. 'Please come, take a seat, we'll show you our plans,' said George cheerfully.

As exciting as this conversation should have been, Arthur couldn't help but look upon the man shouting at the navvies. There was a young boy behind them all. It was David; his school bully was here with him! It couldn't be... he looked just like him; the only difference was he was wearing a spotless suit with a top hat. Arthur jumped down from the oak tree and ran over to the boy juggling with some stones he had found on the floor. 'David?' asked Arthur with little confidence in his voice. 'My name is Henry,' said the boy.

'Oh sorry, you just looked so familiar, I'll leave you alone,' Arthur responded, trying not to anger this clearly important young boy.

'Don't be silly, I admire kids like you, getting your hands dirty every day.' The boy held out his hand. 'Henry Brunel, how do you do?'

Arthur was dumbfounded; this boy was clearly related to David in some sort of way.

'Arthur Morgan,' still shocked but being polite shook, Henry's hand.

Arthur introduced Henry to John, and they were able to chat for a long time while the men figured out how to fix the tunnels. Henry Brunel was at a loss as to why someone so well-spoken and clearly book smart as Arthur, was travelling with these men, who used their muscles a lot more than they use their brains.

'Where are you from Arthur?' asked Henry.

'It's complicated.' replied Arthur miserably.

'Is that your dad then?' asked John, trying his best to change the subject.

'Yes, the engineer who built The Great Western Rail.'

Arthur was astonished once again. 'Your father is Isambard Kingdom Brunel?'

'Yes that's him.' Henry said proudly. 'You really do know a lot don't you Arthur Morgan.'

'It's a long story… can I meet him?' asked Arthur.

'I can ask, but I imagine he's pretty busy, even I don't really get to talk to him much, I had to beg him to come here today and see the tracks. He wasn't sure if it was safe, particularly after yesterday.'

Arthur thought this would be the case, upper-class children rarely spent time with their parents. Most upper-class children during this period spent most of their time with their nannies.

The men were finishing up their business when, without warning, Henry's father starting walking over to the boys.

'Henry, aren't you going to introduce me to your new friends?' said Mr. Brunel.

'Yes father, this is Arthur and John, they're the same age as me, Arthur is one of the most intelligent boys I've ever met.' said Henry. Arthur couldn't help but blush from embarrassment.

'How do you do?' said Mr. Brunel.

'Very well, sir,' said Arthur entirely in awe of the man standing in front of him.

'I'm sure I'll be seeing you boys more often in the next few days. My supervision at this site will be increased hugely after the horrible accident that occurred yesterday.'

Henry was ecstatic. 'Can I come here too?'

'I don't see why not, as long as you stay far away from the men working.'

That's what we have to do too,' said John hypercritically. Henry obviously loved the idea of being around his father, but more importantly, now he had friends to talk to.

Chapter 17

The Invitation

Arthur had spent a full week in 1852 now, as the men finally sat down at the end of a twelve-hour workday, Arthur and John said their goodbyes to Henry for the day. Promising to be back tomorrow, Henry waved goodbye through the small window at the back of Brunel's stagecoach.

'One day Arthur, one day that will be us, just as rich as Henry and we'll be able to ride a stagecoach, and go back to our huge home.' John said enviously.

'Yes, I'm sure it will, John.' said Arthur sounding unusually confident. Arthur seemed in better spirits these days; he still missed home but not the house itself. Mainly, the people, his family, his friends, he spent more time appreciating what he had rather than stressing about the little things. Watching TV, having a mobile phone, and worrying about Miss Madison. He still found it strange looking at Henry, such a wonderfully kind boy, but having the appearance just like David Brunel, his nemesis on the playground.

The sun was beginning to set while Arthur laid down in a trench next to the hut George made for them. Blissfully watching the stars appear out from the darkness. Sat there still in confusion as to how this could even be the same world he lived in, just a lot older. The moonlight was now visible, but Arthur's perception had changed. This was not just some scientific occurrence but a sign, as he looked up at the faint, silvery moon, he started to feel hope, everything was going to be OK.

As morning struck, the men were back at work, and after a full week of picking and digging, the tunnel incident was almost unrecognisable. Sadly, this meant Isambard Kingdom Brunel would no longer have to supervise the men until the next bridge or hill was scheduled, which could be weeks away. This meant Henry could be seeing Arthur and John for the last time, for a very long time. Nevertheless, Arthur was in awe of the way Mr. Brunel conducted his workers, fearless and persistent. Nothing seemed to bother him. He'd often say to the workers, 'the line must be straight, if there is a river, we build a bridge over it, if there is a hill, we must build a tunnel through it.' Arthur admired his spirit and in turn, enjoyed talking with Henry and John. John spent some time catching up to the boy's language, being the only one to not be in school.

'You two still hungry?' said Henry, 'I have some sweet leftover from yesterday,' The boys' eyes sparkled at the thought of any food that was burnt to a crisp on the fire.

'Starving!' said John. The boys sat blissfully watching the horses at the top of the hill.

'Where did you get these, Henry?' asked John.

'Had some spare pocket money my dad let me use at the sweet shop.'

'I miss pocket...' Arthur stopped himself, no working-class child received pocket money in the Victorian times, they'd think he was a liar, or worse crazy!

'How much you get?' said John.

'Not much, couple of shillings a week.' said Henry.

John was shocked, 'oh, wow! That's more than my dad makes!'

Henry felt guilty whereas Arthur was working it out in his head, that's not much more than about £7 a week, Arthur thought. Now Arthur was in shock, but not for the same reason as John. Although Arthur had always considered himself, and his family to not have a lot of money, he was given £5 a week. He couldn't believe it. After all this time, comparing himself to his friends back home, he was getting almost the same amount as an upper-class child in London. This thought made Arthur miserable. How selfish and ungrateful had he been to his parents, every time he asked for more money? Pocket money was never his right, a binding contract his parents must agree to, it was a privilege, one that he only now realised, that he had taken for granted. This was just another one of the countless lessons Arthur was learning since being here. The truth was, Arthur was actually a lot luckier than he first thought he was. One look at John, wolfing down the sweets in front of him, and Arthur couldn't help but think of how blessed he was, to have the memory of being sat down at the dining table, laughing and eating with his brother faced opposite him. Where he had a warm home, hot showers, and a comfy bed to lie down in every night. Arthur muttered the same words he usually did, this for a completely different reason, 'It's not fair.' and for the first time, he wasn't talking about himself. At that moment, all he wanted to do was go home. Not to escape this wretched world, but to take John with him, and give him the same life he has had the pleasure of having. To provide John with the education, he wrongfully missed out on.

The time had come to leave for the day, and as Mr. Brunel was approaching the boys, he noticed the sweet wrappers next to Arthur and John. Without hesitation, he spoke to Henry,

'Well, it looks like you've spent all your pocket money.' Henry thought he was in trouble, but then, he turned to Arthur and John, 'You boys must have been pretty hungry?' The boys all looked guilty, and Arthur and John cowardly nodded their heads in shame.

'What do you boys say we take you back to our cottage down the road, it's not much, but it's temporary while we're building here.' The boys all looked at each other in amazement, the same way Arthur used to look at Tom when his parents agreed to a play date.

'We'd love to Mr. Brunel,' snapped Arthur.

'Then it's settled, I'll clear it with your father and have you accompany us home on the stagecoach.' Said Mr. Brunel.

Within no time, the boys and Brunel were leaving the site to have dinner in a cottage, and Arthur was finally going to have some clean water and a proper meal for the first time in over a week. But more importantly,

John's first time eating a decent meal. Henry was ecstatic; he'd never had friends come over for dinner. He only experienced endless social events with annoying children who desperately wanted to be with the adults in the other room.

Chapter 18

An Upper Class Dinner

For the first time in two weeks, Arthur was able to wash up; all the scrapes and falls he had had, were now being washed off. Falling in the muddy puddle, being thrown into horse manure to name but two. It wasn't quite like having a shower at home but washing away the horrible odour was a massive relief for him. John enjoyed the experience too; playfully using the soap like it was from an alien planet, and using two towels to try himself with, just because he could. The boys were also given fresh clothes from Henry, only the most beautiful waistcoats and bowler hats Henry could offer, which the boys just couldn't say no to. Henry refused to have them sit in the dining room and not stick out like a sore thumb. Tonight, they were not navvying children, but complete equals.

The dining room was beautiful; the table was set with twenty-four china plates setting along with eight forks all assigned to different purposes. Water, wine and a massive loaf of bread were all in attendance. Arthur was amazed, but at the same time, he felt guilty, he couldn't believe this was just a few miles away from all the poverty and homeless people sleeping in the bitter cold. The Brunel family looked terrific, but they weren't the only ones. Another man was sitting beside Mr. Brunel, this man looked slightly older than Brunel, with his hair a little greyer and masking his face the with the same mutton-chopped beard style as Brunel.

'Ah, boys, glad you're ready, I'd like you to meet a friend of mine, this is Robert Stephenson.'

Arthur hadn't met him before but had heard the name Stephenson in history lessons.

'Pleasure to meet you boys,' said Mr. Stephenson, shaking their hands. 'Isambard tells me your fathers a navvy?'

'Mine is, Arthur is my friend who lives with us, he knows everything,' said John.

'Is that right?' said Mr. Stephenson.

'Not everything, just some general things, are you related to George Stephenson?' said Arthur.

'Well yes, that was my father, the father of the railways, as most people know him. I suppose you do know quite a bit, don't you?'

Arthur was blushing, but continued the conversation,

'He invented the steam locomotive, right? If it wasn't for him, there wouldn't be any trains would there?' said Arthur excitedly.

'My word, you certainly do know a lot,' said Mr. Stephenson with a delighted look on his face. Henry was pleased to see he had befriended such impressive dinner guests.

Arthur had to be careful, as intelligent as he was, they would never believe he was from the future, he thought back to the tale Miss Madison told him in class once. A scientist named Galileo almost went to jail, because he discovered that the earth revolved around the sun and that the earth was not the centre of the universe. This was is now common knowledge, but back in 1633, they wanted to arrest him! Arthur couldn't run the risk, the second he mentioned time-travel, he could be treated worse than when he arrived here!

'Tell me, what else do you know about the locomotive?' asked Stephenson.

'Not much, just that your dad invented it, nothing else.' replied Arthur, trying to dumb himself down a little.

'Yes, well he couldn't do it all alone, not without the help of coal, and of course the navvies. My word those men can work, practically inhuman. John felt left out, he was trying to find a good excuse to chime in on the conversation until he blurted it out, 'This all sounds amazing, but I always thought my father was just a navvy because it was something he could do... So we could eat. It's not as if he's building the Houses of Parliament.' The gentlemen were not offended; In fact, they all laughed; they didn't expect ten-year-old boys to understand the importance of these railways.

'Young man,' Mr. Stephenson began 'your father and his colleagues are the unsung heroes of the industrial revolution! They're helping us transport tons of merchandise into London every day. Just think, before railways all we had were horses carrying nowhere near as much as the trains do today, coal, fresh food and people. I mean, there were the canals, we used them for a while to transport these things on boats, but again, not as fast, plus there was the issue of the water freezing during the winter. Trains are helping speed everything along, leaving other countries to play catch-up, and none of this would be possible if it wasn't for the thousands of workers just like your dad braving it out in the cold every day to make it happen, trust me, dear boy, your dad's a hero!' For the first time in his life, John felt overwhelming pride, he wasn't some homeless boy travelling up and down the country living hand to mouth, he was following heroes, and one day he'd become one himself.

Robert continued, 'Yes, I remember the day my father discovered the importance of steam. He said with enough coal, we could change the world, burn the coal, heat the water, produce the steam, steam can push the pistons and there you have it. He made it seem so simple, of course it wasn't!'

Chapter 19

Small World

Arthur loved the conversation over dinner; who needs Miss Madison when you can listen to the actual engineers responsible for building Britain.

'This is so much better than hearing my teacher talk about the locomotives,' said Arthur, slipping up once again about going to school while finishing the last of his desert.

'I wasn't aware you went to school, Mr. Morgan?' asked Mr. Brunel.

Arthur had to think fast, does he make up another weak lie, or come clean and tell the truth, while risking being labelled as a lunatic.

'Well, not really,' said Arthur quietly. 'I... well, I used to, but then... I don't know the man on the front gate said I'm not allowed back anymore.' Arthur really thought about burying his head on the table, and then he just wanted to scream on the top of his lungs the truth about everything. In the end, he settled for yet another murky watered-down version of the truth.

'Oh how strange,' Mr. Brunel began, 'Well you seem to have plenty of knowledge, I'm sure you'll go far no matter what.' Thoughtfully winking at Arthur.

'Well I do miss school, that's for sure, although I don't miss my teacher.'

'No, we don't either,' said Mr. Stephenson, 'horrible species they are aren't they, we had one of the scariest teachers ever to join the profession.'

'Can't be worse than mine,' said Arthur, just as he continued the men took a long-lasting sip of their wine they had in front of them, 'Miss Madison was vicious.'

Both Mr. Stephenson and Mr. Brunel spat out their wine in disbelief, like wide-eyed owls, 'Miss Madison?' yelled both Brunel and Stephenson in unison, 'she taught us when we were at school!'

Arthur was confused, 'how is that possible?'

'Well she was quite young when she taught us,' said Mr. Stephenson, 'no surprise she carried on teaching once we left.'

'She only lives about two miles down the road from here, I'm guessing that's the last person you want to see right now, am I right Arthur' said Mr. Brunel.

That statement could not have been more wrong, Arthur was dying to find out how he landed in this century; Miss Madison could have all the answers. Maybe this was all her fault, a cruel punishment for her least favourite student. Within seconds, countless scenarios played out in his head, all featured Miss Madison as the villain responsible for all his misery. Eventually, he calmed his down and spoke the words he had meant to say.

'I'd love to! Please tell me where and I'll go now!'

Everybody in the room was confused, here Arthur was just seconds before, complaining about this horrible woman, now he wants nothing more than to go to her house.

'Are you sure, Arthur?' said John. 'I thought you liked it here.'

I do, I just, she can help me find my parents.'

The men in the room couldn't understand how this was possible but could see how important it was to Arthur.

'Right, well let me find my address book, and I can lend you my horse-drawn carriage tonight if you wish?' said Mr. Brunel.

Arthur was filled with joy, he felt a sudden nudge, like when you're half asleep dreaming and start to realise this isn't real. Finally, Arthur could see the light at the end of the very long tunnel that he had been travelling through since he had stuck here.

Although this was great news for Arthur, John felt disheartened and confused, which made his headache. This meant Arthur wouldn't be returning to the shantytowns with him. Once the table was cleared, the boys went to Henry's room. Meanwhile, the men sat down in the living room, drinking more wine, while Brunel flicked through his address book. John took Arthur aside away from anyone who could overhear them.

'So you're leaving us?' asked John.

Arthur selfishly didn't even consider leaving the only people in this world that helped him survive, this could be the last time he saw John, even worse, he couldn't say goodbye to George.

'I'm sorry John, this could be my only chance of getting back home, to see my parents, and my brother and my friends... come with me!'

'You're mad! I can't leave, my dad will worry sick, plus I already have everything I'd ever need. I have my dad, my friends, the navvies, and one day I'll be a hero just like them, you heard what Mr. Stephenson said. No, I'm sorry, Arthur, but I can't leave.'

'You have no idea what you're missing John, there's a whole world I want to show you, I can get you new clothes, give you food, and you should see the things people have now.' In his excitement, Arthur was about to mention the wonders of phones, televisions, and video games but managed to contain his enthusiasm.

'I don't care about those things, what good is food if you cant share it with my family. No way, some of these upper-class people have everything but the things that mean the most, friends and family. I tell you what Arthur, some people are so poor, all they have is money.'

John was adamant, which meant Arthur would be making the journey on his own.

Brunel advised he go tomorrow at a more respectable time, but Arthur couldn't wait. Although this evening had been the highlight of his time here, he was dying to return home to his family.

Arthur said his goodbyes to everyone, this time taking John aside, determined to leave on a positive note,

'John I can't thank you enough, you and your dad saved my life, I don't think I would have survived another night if George hadn't found me.'

'It was our pleasure, Arthur. I'll try and explain things to dad, but what's your plan?'

'Get to Miss Madison's house and explain everything. That I've been lost for two weeks and finally found her, and need to get home to my parents, she'll know how to get me back.'

Arthur then said his goodbyes to Henry Brunel, this felt weird, as he would probably be seeing his doppelganger, David, very soon. Arthur wished he could just replace Henry for David. One was so wonderful to be around, whereas the other just made fun of him. Looking forward, Arthur felt anything David did from now on would never compare to the torture he had endured these past few weeks.

Chapter 20

Are We There Yet?

Mr. Brunel sent Arthur on his way in his own stagecoach with Miss Madison's address the destination. He waved goodbye to his friends, not knowing if he'll ever see them again, he was excited, but at the same time apprehensive, Arthur didn't want to get his hopes up, what if this was a completely different Miss Madison? Arthur would have to get back on the horse and go back to the navvies. Arthur was frightened at the thought of spending another night here, now that he'd been giving hope, he didn't want to let go of it. He started to plan on what to say, one positive was that he wasn't turning up with his old school clothes on, covered in horse manure, but in one of Henry's suits and bowler hat. Even if it wasn't the same Miss Madison, he doubted she would handle him the way the horrible men did when he arrived here. But what if it was the same Miss Madison? Would she be angry? Would she even give Arthur a chance to explain? Meanwhile, the stagecoach went over a small ditch, snapping Arthur out of reverie. Plodding along Arthur was getting impatient,

'Are we there yet,' he asked the driver.'

'Oh, not far sir,'

Arthur was too excited; time was going agonizingly slow, then he thought, horses were definitely slower than cars.

Arthur thought back to the long journeys he and his family used to go on, they never really went abroad to other countries. They chose to drive down to the coast in the summer, he remembered complaining about not being able to go to Spain like some of his other friends. Now, sat in the stagecoach, Arthur wanted nothing more than to be in that car right now, travelling down to places so much better than this place, down to Cornwall, where the air is cleaner than the smog covered Victorian London.

The sun was no longer visible as the day turned to night; Arthur felt the temperature change like stepping outside his warm flat during the winter. As they drove through the local village, where the only lights Arthur could see, was the dim gas street lamps. Rocking and rolling out of the town, they travelled through a very narrow man-made footpath amongst the forest. Once the streetlights were no longer visible in the backseat window, Arthur felt worried, what was a warm, bright setting when he started this journey, was now a cold dark, unpredictable night. He folded his arms across his body, rapidly stroking his arms to try and stay warm. Arthur was now starting to regret insisting he travel so soon, would it have made a difference if he had just waited till the morning?

'How much longer?' asked Arthur clearly becoming impatient.

The driver was starting to take offence to Arthur's questions.

'Ten minutes, or so sir, twenty-minute walk if you'd rather go on foot.'

'I'm sorry, just not used to this,' replied Arthur. He took a deep breath and exhaled to try and breathe out all the worries and fears he had held in his head. He started to close his eyes like he did too when his family went on long journeys, sometimes he'd fall asleep and two hours later wake up and arrive in no time. Sadly, the coach wheels and the roads weren't as smooth as his mum's car. Every time he felt himself doze off, the coach would jolt him awake.

Chapter 21

The Highwayman

Suddenly, Arthur heard a huge bang! Like a gunshot going off, it was way too dark for Arthur to see what was happening. At that moment, a face appeared from the window, a scar under his left check, wearing a tricorne hat and holding a pistol. All Arthur could see was this gruesome head bobbing up and down through the window as the stagecoach came to a grinding halt. In the middle of the forest, amongst the cold darkness, stood a man with a pistol, on his horse. This terrifying man was a highwayman, one of many thieves that roamed the country roads at night stalking its victims, usually horse and carriages carrying upper-class rich folk. Sadly for both the highwayman and Arthur, they had very little money between them.

'Give me everything you own rich boy,' said the menacing man.

'I have nothing to give, honest,' pleaded Arthur. He felt his heart in his mouth as he stared up at the man dressed in his red velvet coat and black leather bottoms. Arthur wasn't sure how he would escape this situation alive. He had nothing to give to this highwayman but had so much to lose, all the hope and excitement of seeing his family again was slowly fading away. The driver never said I word. All parties stared at Arthur, assuming he was the wealthiest out of the three of them. If only they knew the truth, that the suit he was wearing was the only thing worth something in this world. No money, no fortune, nothing.

"Get out of the cart... Now!' yelled the highwayman.

The highwayman dragged Arthur by his ankles roughly out of the stagecoach under cover of darkness. Arthur begged him to let him be, but the highwayman was determined not to leave empty-handed. The driver was thrown from the driver's seat and stood in a panic with Arthur; after holding a pistol to them both for quite some time, they emptied their pockets. The driver only had some spare change, which the highwayman snatched from him within seconds, whereas Arthur had the nothing, just a note with Miss Madison's address on it. The highwayman was puzzled and disheartened at this moment, just seconds before he felt like it was Christmas day; a beautiful newly built stagecoach strolling aimlessly through the pathway towards him, with no guards surrounding its owner. An easy moneymaker was now nothing short of a cruel prank. The only item worth anything would be the stagecoach and the horses pulling it.

The highwayman stumbled on to the only stagecoach in London carrying nothing but a poor boy. Therefore, he carefully tied his own horse to the reigns adding him to the front of the coach along with the two horses, and rode away, leaving Arthur and the driver stranded.

'Well, this is just great!' expressed the driver. 'All you had to do is wait until tomorrow, but no, you couldn't. I don't exactly know how you came to find Master Brunel, but if I knew from the start that I'd be driving some homeless kid around the forest at night, I'd of ran for the hills!' He stormed off in the direction back to the cottage. Arthur was left with nothing but Miss Madison's address and plenty of guilt. Goodness knows how long it's going to take the driver to walk back, and if it's even safe.

'I'm so sorry!' Arthur yelled, but the driver seemed like he either didn't hear him or just didn't care for his empty apology.

Arthur was now all alone, with the address to someone with the same name as his teacher, not sure whether it was the same person. Arthur had two choices, play if safe and run after the driver, he'd reluctantly take Arthur back to Brunel explaining the failed trip and the stolen horses, or, risk everything at a small chance

119

of returning home, where he could be with his family, his friends and his own bed. Arthur thought about how good George and John had been to him, and if he was lost, he might never see his family or them ever again. But then he imagined kicking a football around with his dad, his brother James, then Tom and Lucia joining them at the park.

'I have to go,' he whispered to himself. He took off in the opposite direction to his driver and walked on with a purpose to Miss Madison's address.

Chapter 22

Reunion

Arthur started traipsing through the streets of London, which filled him with fear but something strange happened. People were not treating Arthur like the fruit fly in their room; they looked at him with a sense of respect and importance. Arthur had no idea that just wearing a suit could make all the difference, Victorian people were judgmental he thought, one minute he's an annoying little fruit fly, then the next minute, people are begging him for money and tipping their hats off to him. Then he thought back to his mum, the most fantastic person in the world. She gave that homeless man at the train station no time at all, didn't even looked at him, even when the man called out 'have a good day,' Arthur looked around at some of the poor children on the street, 'it's just not fair,' he thought, 'sometimes under the poorest clothes, lies the richest heart.' At that moment, a homeless man approached him, 'any spare change, sir?' the poor man said.

'I'm sorry I have nothing on me, but if I did I'd give you everything, you're a brave man, and I wish you the best for the future, and if we meet again, I promise I'll give you whatever I can spare.' The man was baffled; he'd never had anyone talk to him in such a kind way or shown him this much respect. Arthur may never see this man again, but hoped what he said, at least improved his day.

Miss Madison's house was just in the distance, Arthur was so close, he wanted nothing more than to just get home, to see his family and friends again, to sit by the River Thames and just admire how beautiful London is and how much it has improved from these ghastly times.

Arthur approached the door with apprehension, what if Mr. Brunel was wrong? What if there is a different Miss Madison, like how Henry was not David but a distant relative, this could just be Miss Madison's great grandmother, who was even worse than his own teacher! Arthur was about to knock on this woman's door and ask to be returned to the 21st century. Why didn't he just go back to the navvies with John he thought, now he would be kicked to the curb, in London, lost, and alone once again.

Arthur knocked on the door, timidly, 'Who is it?' snapped the woman behind the door. After a short pause of deafening silence, Arthur spoke, 'It's… Arthur Morgan… I'm looking for Miss-'
'Arthur?' said the woman worriedly. The door was swung open, standing in the doorway was Miss Madison, the very same Miss Madison that had given Arthur plenty of detentions and provided him with lots

of miserable memories. Yet, Arthur could not be happier to see her.

'You fool, what are you doing here?'

'I didn't mean to, I just went to wipe off the date and, and, I,' Arthur broke down right in front of his teacher. Although he was happy to see her, Arthur felt he was finally safe to cry, fear from any judgment and embarrassment.

Miss Madison was beside herself, first with anger, now with empathy, goodness knows how long Arthur had been here. She'd been travelling through time for years but still remembers the fear she had, doing it for the first time.

'Come in, don't worry, everything's going to be alright.'

Chapter 23

Time Travel Lesson

Miss Madison went to get Arthur a drink while Arthur quietly sat in his teacher's living room, this would have been unbelievable to anyone, but what gave Arthur a headache was the photos that surrounded him. The room was full of photographs of countless famous people. Arthur had to stop crying in amazement and look around at the incredible sight in front of him. Miss Madison had pictures of herself with everyone you could dream of, Isaac Newton, Albert Einstein, Barack Obama and many more. 'Miss

Madison, I'm really confused,' said Arthur still wiping away his tears. 'Let me explain,' said Miss Madison, 'the blackboard you touched, it's a magical device used to travel through time. I discovered it when it was put into the classroom many years ago, I wrote the wrong date by accident one day, putting the 29th of September instead of the 30th, I ended up reliving the whole day again. I started to play around with it, just going to certain dates, then, one day, I felt brave; I put 2100 in the date. Sadly, nothing happened, I'm assuming by that point someone had taken the blackboard down and destroyed it. Still, I was able to go as far as 2070, and it worked! From then on, I chose to use the time travelling device for my own curiosity. I have taught everyone you can imagine. First on my list was Albert Einstein, 1890, and then I wanted to see what Martin Luther King was like as a young boy. It only took you back in time, not in a different place, so I had to take a ship to some places like America.'

Arthur's head was hurting, how could this be? And if she only taught famous people, why teach his class.

What brought her to his classroom or who? 'Miss Madison, what made you want to teach my class?'

'Oh Arthur, I can't tell you that, all I can say is I always travel in time to teach people the fundamentals, so they can then go on to change the world.' Arthur was intrigued, someone in his class was going to change the world, in some sort of way, but who was it? Tom? David? Himself? Only time would tell.

'Where have you been hiding then since being here, clearly done well for yourself from the look of your clothes.' said Miss Madison.

'Well it's been pretty rough, spent a night on the street which was the worst night of my life! But then I found George, he's a navvy, he had a son the same age as me, I've spent most of my time with them,'

'Sounds like George may have saved your life! But navvies don't own suits.'

'No this is Henry Brunel's, his dad gave me this suit, gave me your address, you know, Isambard Kingdom Brunel.' Arthur said proudly.

'Ah yes another great mind I've had the pleasure of knowing, so how long have you been stuck here?'

'I'm not sure. What's the date today? All I know is that I rubbed the date 23rd of May 1852,'

'What!' Miss Madison yelled, dropping her glass of water in the process. After a smash of glass hit the floor, Miss Madison grabbed Arthur's hand.

'No, no, no, this can't be! Arthur, we need to get you home this instant.' Miss Madison was panicking, 'I thought you were going to say a couple of days, do you have any idea what diseases you're prone to catching here. Just from drinking the Thames water here, you could get Cholera, Typhoid and lots more! Come on, let's get you back right now!'

Arthur was rushed off his feet, he just wanted to lie down and sleep, but the urge to see his family once again, gave just enough energy to suck it up and follow Miss Madison to the door.

Chapter 24

Back To School

Off they went, racing through the streets of London to get back to the school, to get back to that classroom, to get back home. Arthur was scared out of his mind, what if he had been sick? He couldn't thank the friends he encountered enough for getting him food and keeping him alive. 'Miss Madison wait, I need you to do one more thing when I leave,'

'Never mind anything right now, there's just one thing to worry about, and that's getting you home safe.'

'Just listen,' said Arthur, stopping dead in the middle of the street in protest, 'you need to find George and

John, Mr. Brunel will know who they are, please explain… tell them…' Arthur couldn't expect Miss Madison to tell them the whole story, 'just tell them I said thank you,'

'Alright, I will, I promise, now let's get moving.'

Once they got to the doors, there was no one guarding the outside. Miss Madison held Arthur's hand tightly while she got her keys out from her pocket. Unlocking the building to the front gates brought Arthur closer and closer to his family. Through the dark and dusty halls, they ran, Miss Madison, dragging Arthur so fast he was practically hovering off the ground. They opened then slammed the door shut behind them. Arthur had made it back to the same place he had been just a couple weeks back, only this felt like months ago. Miss Madison ran over to the blackboard, 'when did you say you came here?'

'23rd of May'

'Ok let's go back to the 23rd of May. What time?'

'It was just after detention, I went back to get my bag.'

Miss Madison felt a surge of guilt in her stomach, she was sure that was the day she just couldn't wait for Fern, the caretaker to come and rub the date off. She wrote the exact day Arthur had left to come to 1852 only this time adding the time, 'this should send you straight back, just five minutes after you left, it will feel like you never left, no one will even know you were gone, apart from us two of course,' she then winked at Arthur and grabbed a chair from under one of the desks.

It was finally time to return. Unable to resist giving Miss Madison a hug as a thank you for saving his life, they then said goodbye to each other, ignoring the irony that Arthur hated Miss Madison not too long ago. Arthur stepped onto the chair in front of the blackboard, just like he did before. As Arthur went to wipe away the date, he looked back at Miss Madison and politely said 'See you tomorrow Miss,' with a smile on his face. Arthur saw the same bright light and screaming sounds, only this time, he didn't panic; he didn't guard his ears with his hands. This time he knew what was happening and where he was going; he was going home.

Miss Madison stood by, now replacing the role of Neil, the caretaker. She took the eraser from the shelf and rubbed out the date. She went to leave the room and return home until tomorrow where she'd be seeing Arthur once again.

Chapter 25

Home

Forced to close his eyes due to the blinding light, Arthur waited for everything to stop. Within seconds, everything was silent. Arthur slowly opened his eyes and rubbed them just to make sure he wasn't dreaming. Arthur Morgan never thought he would be so happy to see Miss Madison's classroom again. He looked around and saw the same room that used to bring him fear and anxiety, but now, all he could feel was a sense of joy. As empty as the walls may seem, it would never compare to the room Arthur had just left behind. He took a long deep breath and no longer found himself coughing from the stench of the River Thames or from the smoky skies. This was where Arthur belonged.

Arthur looked down in amazement as his bag was still there, on the floor, waiting for him. He picked it up and ran down the hallway, only this time he was running in Henry's suit and bowler hat, bursting through the doors of the building with a huge smile on his face. Arthur ran through the school gates just in time to say thank you to Fern, the caretaker. 'Thanks, Miss,' said Arthur.

'Thought you were getting your bag, not getting changed for some fancy dress party,' Arthur couldn't help but laugh as he ran the rest of the way home. Arthur ignored all the funny looks from everyone as he weaved in and out wearing Henry's expensive suit. Sadly, his hat came loose from his head and fell off while he ran past the train station, he thought about running to retrieve it, but he just wanted to get home as soon as he could. Arthur came running up the stairs to his front door, finally home, he burst through the doors.

'Mum! Dad! James!' shouted Arthur. All of them sitting down watching TV like Arthur had never been gone, because, to them, he arrived just home thirty minutes later than he usually did. Arthur darted over to them and jumped on them all, he began to cry, not out of sadness but of pure happiness. 'I've missed you all so much,' said Arthur. His family not quite sure what he meant but gladly accepted his greetings with open arms.

'Arthur, what on earth are you wearing?' asked his dad, sounding just like George with his strong Irish accent.

'Trust me, it's a long, long story!' replied Arthur.

'Guess what Arthur! I won my race today!' said James proudly.

'Well done!' Arthur was so happy for him he couldn't help but hold him tighter than he'd either held his at times, annoying little brother. He held his family tighter than ever, Arthur realised, this was more important than any phone or anything else his parents could buy him, being safe with them, away from the cold streets and the feeling of an empty stomach.

After a short while, Arthur's dad had to leave for work, they said goodbye for now. Arthur made his way to the kitchen, shelves full, fridge beaming with food everywhere, he had eaten not too long ago with Mr. Brunel and Mr. Stephenson, but he couldn't resist more food, going hungry for as long as he was meant Arthur could eat for hours and not get full. Although the food was delicious, one thing stood out more than anything. Arthur carefully poured himself a glass of blackcurrant squash, he began to sip, but couldn't help gulp down an entire glass once the juice hit his taste buds. Clean, freshwater, something Arthur took for granted but never again. When he had gone almost two weeks without fresh water, he couldn't care about what video games he didn't have, what his friends were saying in the group chat he wasn't apart of, all he cared about was getting some fresh water. That was the ultimate dream back in the Victorian era for boys on the streets.

Before bed, Arthur needed to have a shower, not a wash like he had at the Brunel cottage but a hot, soaped up shower. Arthur turned the shower on; let it heat up before stepping in then, then put slowly put his head under the shower. This evening was turning out to be one of the best evenings of Arthur had ever had in his life. Although nothing had changed on the outside, Arthur's perspective on what was truly important had changed entirely. As the hot water splashed against his skin, he felt his entire body heat up, washing off all the freezing cold nights he had spent in that horrible place. Eventually, Arthur had used up all the hot water and had to step out.

Arthur Morgan lay down in his bed that night, pondering about the last few weeks, he was so exhausted all he could do was be thankful, he was finally sleeping in his warm, comfortable bed and had a roof over his head.

Chapter 26

Same Day, New Attitude

Arthur woke up just in time to hear his mum coming into his room, 'Come on, boys, time for school,' they both jumped out of bed, excited for the day ahead. Arthur had missed being at school. He just wanted to see his friends again, play football at lunchtime and talk to Tom and Lucia again. They started eating breakfast, Arthur, faster than usual to get to school as early as possible. Moments later, their dad walked through the door from work again, instead of staring down and complaining about a stomach ache, Arthur launched out of his chair and gave his dad a big hug.

'Dad, you know my pocket money?' asked Arthur.

'Yes,' replied dad worriedly.

'Can I have it all now, I want to take it to school, please?'

'I don't know if that a good idea, it's a lot of money for some people.'

'Exactly, to some people, it's a huge amount!'

'What's it for?'

'Again, it's a long, long story, I'll tell you everything later!'

Arthur's dad was felt concerned but knew Arthur wouldn't do anything silly with this much money, He handed Arthur all his pocket money for this month.

'Thank you so much, you have no idea how happy this is going to make me,'

Once they left, Arthur's mum was struggling to keep up with both of them way ahead, 'Slow down, you two, my legs don't move that fast!' said mum. They both ran ahead anyway, racing each other to the end of each road, where they would eventually wait for their mum to catch up before crossing. Passing the station, the same homeless man was sat on the same piece of cardboard he had yesterday.

'Any spare change Miss?' asked the man sat with his legs folded, with a cap upside down with just a few 10p coins in it.

'Not today I'm—'

'Here you go,' said Arthur, interrupting his mum, 'I hope you have a great day; tomorrow I'll try and bring some spare blankets. Pretty cold out here at night times aren't they.'

The man was in shock, Arthur had handed him more money than the man had ever been given by anyone he begged.

'Thank you so much, bless you, bless you and your whole family.' Arthur's mum was confused and proud at the same time. What had happened to her son yesterday? James wanted to laugh; now, he had more money than his older brother. They all walk joyfully away from the station towards school.

'Hey Arthur,' said James, 'I richer than you now, how do you feel,' giggling to himself.'

'We're both rich James. We have the best parents, the greatest friend, get to go school, and have a home just by the river. Sadly, James, some people are so poor, all they have is money.' Echoing the words of John.

Arthur was just in time for the bell to go, but something was different; instead of a smile and a quick nod to his mum and James, he gave them both a big hug and kissed his mum on the cheek. He couldn't care less about looking cool anymore, all he wanted to do was show his mum how much he loved them. He ran over to catch up to Tom, 'Oh my, you have no idea he glad I am to see you again!' said Arthur

'You not mad about me not knocking for you this weekend?'

'Oh, no way! I completely forgot about that, just hope you can make it this weekend?' asked Arthur.

'Sure, can't wait for this week to be over, and it's only Tuesday, feels like this weeks been going on forever.'

Arthur couldn't help but laugh, 'Tell me about it!'

Chapter 27

Letter From An Old Friend

'Morning everyone,' said Miss Madison, looking a bit more cheerful than usual. After the register was taken, Miss Madison went through what the day would include. At this point, Arthur couldn't help but look around. Which one of his classmates would be the next Albert Einstein? The next Isaac Newton?

He looked around and saw the potential they all had, some were leaning back on their chairs, some sat up straight showing complete attention to Miss Madison out of fear of being shouted at.

'Arthur, are you listening?' Miss Madison yelled, snapping him out of his daydream.

David smiled at Arthur's misfortune, but Arthur didn't care, only sad part was that when he looked at David, he missed Henry more than ever. Hopefully, in time, he could get to know David just like he did Henry, and then realise they're not so different, no matter how much money their families had.

'Right, before we begin, let's have the homework in, Thomas? I hope you managed to finish it last night?' asked Miss Madison.

'Yes Miss,' replied Tom miserably,'

'Good work, Arthur?'

Arthur panicked; he got home last night and was so happy to be home he completely forgot to get his homework done.

'Umm... not quite, sorry miss I didn't have time,' said Arthur, holding back his laughter in the irony, time was the one thing he did have.

'Detention again for you then Mr Morgan.'

Arthur couldn't believe it, after everything he went through, to come back to receive a detention, absolutely ridiculous! Arthur could have written what it was like growing up in the Victorian era in less than an hour! He just lived it! But just before Arthur Morgan was about to utter the words 'it's not fair,' one thought crossed his mind, 'I suppose there were worse places to be than in detention.'

The end of the day came, and it was time for Arthur to report to detention, slightly less bothered about it compare to yesterday, Arthur got to Miss Madison's classroom and could see it was just he on his own.

'Is it just me today, Miss?' asked Arthur.

'Yes, I'm sorry, Arthur, you're not in trouble. I just needed to see you alone, first of all, I hope you haven't told anyone about what happened to you?'

'Not yet, I was going to tell my parents tonight,'

'Don't worry about that, I've called them, they are coming in tonight for a parents meeting, it was my mistake, and I need to be the one to tell them.'

'OK, thank you I guess,' Arthur was relieved, he thought his family would laugh at the whole made-up story and call him crazy.

'One more thing, Arthur, before you go,' Miss Madison approached him with a letter, 'this is from John; please don't mention any of this from now on. I'd like to put this whole situation behind us and continue changing lives for the better.' Arthur thought he'd be angry at Miss Madison, but he wasn't, he wanted to thank her, as horrible as the whole experience was, he saw his life with such colour now, so much hope and appreciation like never before.

Arthur nodded in agreement and left the classroom, on his way home, sat by the river, and finally opened the letter.

Dear Arthur,

I still can't write very well, so I'm just talking to your teacher while she writes everything down. Things have changed quite a lot since you've been gone. It's been about seven years now since you left. My dad has had to retire, too old for all the heavy lifting. I've just started to get permission to go into the tunnels; I still see Henry and Mr Brunel from time to time. Thank you for everything, even though it was such a short time, you taught me so much. I hope you're doing well and are safe and sound with your family, but most of all, I hope you are happy. Don't worry too much about us, we're still eating and living well, and now that I'm allowed to help out with the navvies I can proudly say I am one now. As hard as the work is, I get to sleep at night and think about what Mr Stephenson said all those years ago. Navvies are the unsung heroes of building Britain! What I'm trying to say Arthur is this; I'm truly living the dream.

Sincerely,
John

Arthur was amazed, even with just a plate of meat and a small hut to return to every day, John seemed just as happy as one of the wealthiest footballers around. This proved the point Arthur had been thinking about all day since he returned home. Being happy has nothing to do with having everything you want, it's about appreciating all the things you already have.

Printed in Great Britain
by Amazon